Dear Parent:

Congratulations! Your child is taking the first steps on an exciting journey. The destination? Independent reading!

STEP INTO READING® will help your child get there. The program offers books at five levels that accompany children from their first attempts at reading to reading success. Each step includes fun stories, fiction and nonfiction, and colorful art. There are also Step into Reading Sticker Books, Step into Reading Math Readers, Step into Reading Write-In Readers, Step into Reading Phonics Readers, and Step into Reading Phonics First Steps! Boxed Sets—a complete literacy program with something to interest every child.

Learning to Read, Step by Step!

Ready to Read Preschool–Kindergarten
• big type and easy words • rhyme and rhythm • picture clues
For children who know the alphabet and are eager to begin reading.

Reading with Help Preschool–Grade 1
• basic vocabulary • short sentences • simple stories
For children who recognize familiar words and sound out new words with help.

Reading on Your Own Grades 1–3
• engaging characters • easy-to-follow plots • popular topics
For children who are ready to read on their own.

Reading Paragraphs Grades 2–3
• challenging vocabulary • short paragraphs • exciting stories
For newly independent readers who read simple sentences with confidence.

Ready for Chapters Grades 2–4
• chapters • longer paragraphs • full-color art
For children who want to take the plunge into chapter books but still like colorful pictures.

STEP INTO READING® is designed to give every child a successful reading experience. The grade levels are only guides. Children can progress through the steps at their own speed, developing confidence in their reading, no matter what their grade.

Remember, a lifetime love of reading starts with a single step!

To Ruby, who will always be my first princess
—J.L.W.

www.stepintoreading.com

Educators and librarians, for a variety of teaching tools, visit us at www.randomhouse.com/teachers

Library of Congress Cataloging-in-Publication Data
Weinberg, Jennifer.
What is a princess? / by Jennifer Liberts Weinberg.
    p. cm. — (Step into reading. A step 1 book)
Summary: Simple text and illustrations describe the qualities shared by some of Disney's princesses, including Snow White, Belle, Cinderella, Jasmine, and Ariel.
ISBN 0-7364-2238-2 — ISBN 0-7364-8030-7 (lib.bdg)
[1. Princesses—Fiction. 2. Disney characters—Fiction.] I. Title. II. Series: Step into reading. Step 1 book.
PZ7.W436135 Wh 2004 [E]—dc22 2003021143

Printed in the United States of America   40 39 38 37 36

STEP INTO READING, RANDOM HOUSE, and the Random House colophon are registered trademarks of Random House, Inc.

What Is a Princess?

by Jennifer Liberts Weinberg
illustrated by Atelier Philippe Harchy

Random House 🏠 New York

What is a princess?

A princess is kind.

Snow White gives
Grumpy a big kiss.

A princess is smart.
Belle reads
lots of books.

A princess is caring.
Belle helps the Beast
when he is hurt.

A princess likes
to dress up.

Cinderella wears

a gown . . .

. . . and glass slippers.

What is a princess?

A princess is brave.

Jasmine stands up
to the evil Jafar.

A princess is
ready for fun.

Jasmine flies
through the sky.

A princess loves
to see new things.

Ariel finds

a sunken ship.

A princess is
a dreamer.

Ariel wishes to
go on land.

What is a princess?
A princess is polite.

"Thank you,"
says Briar Rose.

A princess loves to sing and dance.

And a princess
always lives
happily ever after!